MR.SMALL

by Roger Hargreaves

KU-631-454

Mr Small was very small. Probably the smallest person you've ever seen in your whole life.

Or perhaps the smallest person you've never seen in your whole life, because he was so small you probably wouldn't see him anyway.

Mr Small was about as big as a pin, which isn't very big at all, so perhaps we should say that Mr Small was as small as a pin!

Mr Small lived in a small house underneath a daisy at the bottom of Mr Robinson's garden.

It was a very nice house, although very tiny, and it suited Mr Small very well indeed. He liked living there.

Now, this story is all about the time Mr Small decided to get a job.

The trouble was, what sort of job could Mr Small do? After all there aren't that many small jobs!

Mr Small had thought about it for a long time, but hadn't had any ideas.

Not one!

He was thinking about it now, while he was having lunch.

He was having half a pea, one crumb, and a drop of lemonade.

After he'd rested for a while Mr Small set off again and walked all of the rest of the way to Mr Robinson's house without stopping once.

When he got there he climbed up the steps to Mr Robinson's back door.

He knocked at the door.

Nobody heard him!

He knocked again at the door.

Nobody heard him!

The trouble was, you see, that if you're as small as Mr Small you don't have a very loud knock.

Mr Small looked up.

There, high above his head, was a doorbell.

"How can I ring the bell when I can't reach it?" thought Mr Small to himself.

He started to climb up the wall, brick by brick, to reach the bell.

He had climbed up four bricks when he made the mistake of looking down.

"Oh dear," he said, and fell.

Bang!!

"Ouch!" said Mr Small, rubbing his head.

Just then Mr Small heard footsteps.

It was the postman.

The postman came to the door, posted his letters, and was just about to leave when he heard a voice.

"Hello," said the voice.

The postman looked down.

"Hello," he said to Mr Small. "Who are you?"

"I'm Mr Small," said Mr Small. "Will you ring the bell for me?"

"Of course I will," replied the postman in answer to Mr Small's question, and reaching out he pressed the bell with his finger.

"Thank you," said Mr Small.

"My pleasure," said the postman, and off he went.

Mr Small heard footsteps coming to the door.

The door opened.

Mr Robinson opened the door and looked out.

"That's funny," he said. "I'm sure I heard somebody ring the bell!"

He was about to shut the door when he heard a little voice.

"Hello," said the voice. "Hello, Mr Robinson."

Mr Robinson looked down, and down.

"Hello," he said. "What are you doing here?"

"I've come to ask your advice," said Mr Small to Mr Robinson.

"Well," said Mr Robinson. "You'd better come in and have a talk."

Mr Small followed Mr Robinson into the house, and, perched on the arm of Mr Robinson's favourite chair, he told him how he couldn't think of a job that he could do.

Mr Robinson sipped a cup of tea, and listened.

"So you see," Mr Small explained, "how difficult it is."

"Yes, I can see that," said Mr Robinson. "But leave it to me!"

Mr Robinson knew a lot of people.

Mr Robinson knew somebody who worked in a restaurant, and arranged for Mr Small to work there.

Putting mustard into mustard pots!

But Mr Small kept falling into the pots and getting covered in mustard, so he left that job.

Mr Robinson knew somebody who worked in a sweetshop, and arranged for Mr Small to work there.

Serving sweets!

But Mr Small kept falling into the sweet jars, so he left that job.

Mr Robinson knew somebody who worked in a place where they made matches, and arranged for Mr Small to work there.

Packing matches into boxes!

But Mr Small kept getting shut in the boxes with the matches, so he left that job.

Mr Robinson knew somebody who worked on a farm, and arranged for Mr Small to work there.

Sorting out the brown eggs from the white eggs!

But Mr Small kept getting trapped by the eggs, so he left that job.

"What are we going to do with you?" Mr Robinson asked Mr Small one evening.

"Don't know!" said Mr Small in a small voice.

"I've got one more idea," said Mr Robinson. "I know somebody who writes children's books. Perhaps you could work for him."

So, the following day Mr Robinson took Mr Small to meet the man who wrote children's books.

"Can I work for you?" Mr Small asked the man.

"Yes you can," replied the man. "Pass me that pencil and tell me all about the jobs you've been doing. Then I'll write a book about it. I'll call it *Mr Small*," he added.

"But children won't want to read a book all about me!" exclaimed Mr Small.

"Yes they will," replied the man. "They'll like it very much!"

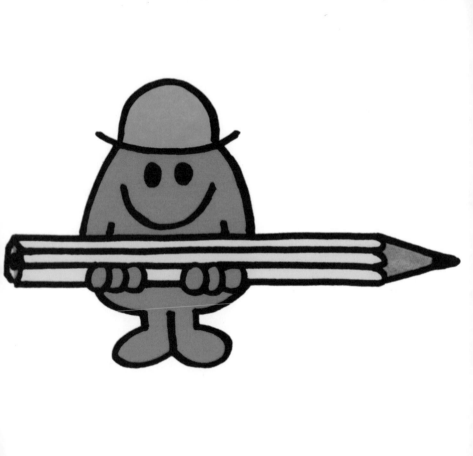

And you did.

Didn't you?

CUT ALONG DOTTED LINE AND RETURN THIS WHOLE PAGE

3 Great Offers for MR.MEN Fans!

MR. MEN TOKEN

1 New Mr. Men or Little Miss Library Bus Presentation Cases

A brand new stronger, roomier school bus library box, with sturdy carrying handle and stay-closed fasteners.

The full colour, wipe-clean boxes make a great home for your full collection.

They're just £5.99 inc P&P and free bookmark!

☐ MR. MEN ☐ LITTLE MISS (please tick and order overleaf)

2 Door Hangers and Posters

In every Mr. Men and Little Miss book like this one, you will find a special token. Collect 6 tokens and we will send you a brilliant Mr. Men or Little Miss poster and a Mr. Men or Little Miss double sided full colour bedroom door hanger of your choice. Simply tick your choice in the list and tape a 50p coin for your two items to this page.

PLEASE STICK YOUR 50P COIN HERE

Door Hangers (please tick)
☐ Mr. Nosey & Mr. Muddle
☐ Mr. Slow & Mr. Busy
☐ Mr. Messy & Mr. Quiet
☐ Mr. Perfect & Mr. Forgetful
☐ Little Miss Fun & Little Miss Late
☐ Little Miss Helpful & Little Miss Tidy
☐ Little Miss Busy & Little Miss Brainy
☐ Little Miss Star & Little Miss Fun

Posters (please tick)
☐ MR.MEN
☐ LITTLE MISS

3 Sixteen Beautiful Fridge Magnets – any **2** for £**2.00**!
inc.P&P

They're very special collector's items!
Simply tick your first and second* choices from the list below
of any 2 characters!

1st Choice
- [ ] Mr. Happy
- [ ] Mr. Lazy
- [ ] Mr. Topsy-Turvy
- [ ] Mr. Bounce
- [ ] Mr. Bump
- [ ] Mr. Small
- [ ] Mr. Snow
- [ ] Mr. Wrong
- [ ] Mr. Daydream
- [ ] Mr. Tickle
- [ ] Mr. Greedy
- [ ] Mr. Funny
- [ ] Little Miss Giggles
- [ ] Little Miss Splendid
- [ ] Little Miss Naughty
- [ ] Little Miss Sunshine

2nd Choice
- [ ] Mr. Happy
- [ ] Mr. Lazy
- [ ] Mr. Topsy-Turvy
- [ ] Mr. Bounce
- [ ] Mr. Bump
- [ ] Mr. Small
- [ ] Mr. Snow
- [ ] Mr. Wrong
- [ ] Mr. Daydream
- [ ] Mr. Tickle
- [ ] Mr. Greedy
- [ ] Mr. Funny
- [ ] Little Miss Giggles
- [ ] Little Miss Splendid
- [ ] Little Miss Naughty
- [ ] Little Miss Sunshine

*Only in case your first choice is out of stock.

--- TO BE COMPLETED BY AN ADULT ---

To apply for any of these great offers, ask an adult to complete the coupon below and send it with the appropriate payment and tokens, if needed, to MR. MEN OFFERS, PO BOX 7, MANCHESTER M19 2HD

- [ ] Please send ____ Mr. Men Library case(s) and/or ____ Little Miss Library case(s) at £5.99 each inc P&P
- [ ] Please send a poster and door hanger as selected overleaf. I enclose six tokens plus a 50p coin for P&P
- [ ] Please send me ____ pair(s) of Mr. Men/Little Miss fridge magnets, as selected above at £2.00 inc P&P

Fan's Name _____

Address _____

_____ **Postcode** _____

Date of Birth _____

Name of Parent/Guardian _____

Total amount enclosed £ _____

- [ ] **I enclose a cheque/postal order payable to Egmont Books Limited**
- [ ] **Please charge my MasterCard/Visa/Amex/Switch or Delta account** (delete as appropriate)

Card Number

Expiry date __/__ **Signature** _____

MR.MEN LITTLE MISS
Mr. Men and Little Miss™ ©Mrs. Roger Hargreaves

Please allow 28 days for delivery. Offer is only available while stocks last. We reserve the right to change the terms of this offer at any time and we offer a 14 day money back guarantee. This does not affect your statutory rights. Data Protection Act: If you do not wish to receive other similar offers from us or companies we recommend, please tick this box [ ]. Offers apply to UK only.

CUT ALONG DOTTED LINE AND RETURN THIS WHOLE PAGE